Zoë
the Tooth Fairy

First published in Great Britain in 2000
by Piccadilly Press Ltd.,
5 Castle Road, London NW1 8PR
www.piccadillypress.co.uk

Text designed by Louise Millar
Printed and bound in Belgium by Proost

ISBN: 1 85340 651 1 (paperback)
EAN: 9 781853 406515

5 7 9 10 8 6

A catalogue record of this book
is available from the British Library

Jane Andrews has two sons and lives in High Wycombe in Buckinghamshire.
She has written nine books for Piccadilly Press
including the eight Zoë titles and MILLY AT MAGIC SCHOOL.

The complete Zoë series:

Find out more at www.piccadillypress.co.uk

Zoë
the Tooth Fairy

Jane Andrews

Piccadilly Press • London

It was prize day at Fairy School. Zoë and Pip and their friends had all passed the Tooth Fairy exams. The Fairy Queen gave them each a beautiful sash. "Well done," she said. "Ms Tooth Fairy and myself are very proud of you. Now you are all tooth fairies. You start tonight."

At last it was dark. The fairies set off in pairs. The Fairy Queen gave them coins to exchange for the children's teeth, little packets of sleep-dust, and maps to show the houses the fairies were to visit that night.

Zoë and Pip had trouble
reading their map.
"This is Mr Owl's house," said Zoë.
"That can't be right!"

They flew on through the dark trees.
But they were flying in circles.
"To-whit! To-woo," said Mr Owl.
"Go that way!"

At last Zoë and Pip found the right house.
They flew up to the bedroom window.
But it was only open a crack, and Zoë got stuck!

"Oh dear, I've forgotten the spell
to make myself small!" she cried.
"Me too," said Pip, pulling Zoë free.
"Never mind. We'll find another way in."

"Here's a funny little door," said Zoë, swooping down
to the ground. "We can get in here." She pushed hard
at the door and the fairies dived straight in.

They both landed in a heap on the other side.

They were in the kitchen. But there was also a cat in
the kitchen! Fortunately for Zoë and Pip it was asleep
in its basket.
"Keep very quiet," whispered Zoë to Pip as they
fluttered past.

Feeling very nervous, Zoë and Pip started to fly up
the stairs. But *then* Pip's sash got caught in the
bannisters. When Zoë tried to help pull her free,
Pip dropped the coin! It rolled down the stairs
and on to the hallway floor, making an awful noise.

"Hiss!" The cat woke up. It chased up
the stairs after Zoë and Pip.
"Help!" cried Pip.
Quickly Zoë threw the sleep-dust into the cat's eyes.
"Phew, that was close," she said, as Pip grabbed the
coin from the hallway floor.

At last Zoë and Pip found their way to the bedroom.
"Where's the tooth?" said Pip.
"Shhh," whispered Zoë. "We mustn't make any noise!
I've thrown all the sleep-dust at the cat! We . . ."

Suddenly the alarm clock next to the bed started ringing!
"Quick! Drop the coin, Pip, we must go!" cried Zoë.

Together Zoë and Pip pushed the bedroom window hard
and it opened just enough for them to get through.
Away they flew into the dawn.

Back at Fairy School, Zoë and Pip told the Fairy Queen about their adventures. They explained how they had got into the house, passed the cat, left the money and escaped through the bedroom window when the alarm clock rang. "Well done, how brave you were!" said the Fairy Queen with a big smile. "Now there is just one more thing – where is the tooth?"

"The tooth!" Zoë looked at Pip, and Pip looked at Zoë,
and they both turned very pink . . .